CUENTO DE LUZ

To Joaquín, with love.

— Sonja Wimmer & Ariel Andrés Almada —

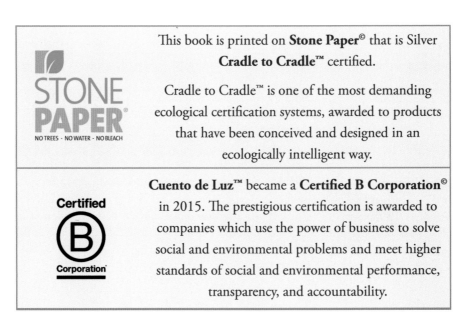

This book is printed on **Stone Paper**© that is Silver **Cradle to Cradle**™ certified.

Cradle to Cradle™ is one of the most demanding ecological certification systems, awarded to products that have been conceived and designed in an ecologically intelligent way.

STONE PAPER®
NO TREES · NO WATER · NO BLEACH

Certified B Corporation

Cuento de Luz™ became a **Certified B Corporation**© in 2015. The prestigious certification is awarded to companies which use the power of business to solve social and environmental problems and meet higher standards of social and environmental performance, transparency, and accountability.

Son
Series: *Family Love*
Text © 2020 Ariel Andrés Almada
Illustrations © 2020 Sonja Wimmer
This edition © 2020 Cuento de Luz SL
Calle Claveles, 10 | Urb. Monteclaro | Pozuelo de Alarcón | 28223 | Madrid | Spain
www.cuentodeluz.com
Original title in Spanish: *Hijo*
English translation by Jon Brokenbow
ISBN: 978-84-18302-17-6
1st printing
Printed in PRC by Shanghai Cheng Printing Company September 2020, print number 1819-6

SON

Ariel Andrés Almada & Sonja Wimmer

Last night, I had a dream. A dream in which you arrived at our home with your eyes open wide, and countless questions deep inside your little heart.

You looked at me, you smiled, and you grabbed my finger
with your tiny hand, as if you were asking me to show
you the whole wide world.

I wake up today, son, and see that nothing is a dream.
That your little body is next to me, and that showing you
all about this world is my most wonderful privilege.

So, where do I start? I'd like to tell you about so many things . . .

About a sky in which there are more stars than grains of sand on all of the Earth's beaches. About how the sunflowers turn to face the sun's rays, while the fireflies make friends at night.

About the sea snails who dance to and fro with the tides, and the bees who work hard every day to make their delicious honey.

I'd like to show you the seasons, and tell you about my favorite . . .

To sit with you in front of a map, and travel across all of the countries with my fingertip, as if distances and frontiers meant nothing at all.

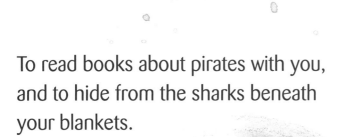

To read books about pirates with you,
and to hide from the sharks beneath
your blankets.

There are so many things for you to discover! Look at the horizon stretching before you . . .

If you put one of your little feet in front of the other, you'll be able to walk all the way around the world.

You'll see places where children travel on sleds pulled by dogs . . . and you will have to wrap up as warm as you can, because the winter is oh so cold!

Countries where the sky is full
of dancing colored lights . . .
countries that are as far north
as you can go!

Deserts, where the storms
bring sand instead of rain . . .
you'll need to wear a scarf to
cover your head!

Mountains that are so high,
they seem to tickle the sky . . .
and if you decide to climb them,
be careful of all that ice!

There are so many roads for you to travel, you'll feel that there aren't enough days in the year. Some of these roads will be smooth, while others will be as rocky as can be.

And you'll need to know that on other roads, behind the rocks, there are sometimes dragons.

But don't worry, son. I think that they are there to help teach us something.

Maybe, if you just keep on walking, even if you're scared, that fear will just get smaller and smaller, until it finally disappears for good.

And if the night should suddenly fall? Well, just stay calm. You'll feel sad, and you'll want to lower your eyes to the ground. But I promise you that if you're brave and you look up, the stars will help to guide you on your way.

But if any time the night is so
dark that you can't even see the
moonlight, then remember to look
deep within yourself, as there is no
better compass than your heart.

My son, I hope that you hear these words as you march along. And maybe, at some point, you'll even start to let go of my hand.

Well, that's just fine. It's only natural. We're made of dreams, and within us we all have the dream to spread our wings and fly away.

But I also know that when you finally do, as high and majestic as an eagle, there will be times when you'll want to look back, to remember where you came from, and exactly where you're heading . . .

And that's where I'll be, always by your side along the way, looking on with a heart full of joy, at the wonderful son you've become.